The Haunted Hayride

Written by Judy Katschke
Illustrated by Prescott Hill

Scholastic Inc.

HASBRO and its logo, BLYTHE, LITTLEST PET SHOP, and all related characters are trademarks of Hasbro and are used with permission. © 2015 Hasbro. All Rights Reserved.

All rights reserved. Published by Scholastic Inc., *Publishers since 1920.* SCHOLASTIC and associated logos are trademarks and/or registered trademarks of Scholastic Inc.

ISBN 978-0-545-85568-6

10 9 8 7 6 5 4 3 2 1   15 16 17 18 19

Printed in the U.S.A.   40
First printing 2015

Contents

Chapter 1
Fall Hay-Day

"Fall is the most awesome season!" Blythe Baxter said as she pedaled through Downtown City Park. Her bike was hitched to a wagon filled with

hay and *pets*! "Fall means apple cider, crunchy leaves, and hayrides!"

"Hayrides mean hay fever!" Sunil the mongoose sneezed. *"Achooo!"*

The Littlest Pet Shop day-campers were having a blast on their first fall hayride. They were also dressed head to tail in Blythe Style, Blythe's very own line of pet fashions.

Blythe had a special knack for designing pet clothes. She also had a *secret* knack: She could talk to animals!

"Don't forget," Blythe called back. "We're looking for ideas for Littlest Pet Shop's fall window display so keep your eyes peeled."

"Like bananas?" Minka the monkey cried. "Where are they? *Wheeeeeerrrre?*"

Thanks to Mrs. Twombly, the store's owner, Blythe had permission to keep the pets out later than usual that day, as long as they were back before dark.

"I always did like the nightlife!" Vinnie said, kicking up hay with some fancy footwork. "And I'm not even nocturnal!"

Suddenly, Blythe screeched to a stop as something big, round, and orange rolled in front of her bike.

"What the yikes!" Blythe cried.

"Fall also means pumpkins," Russell the hedgehog said.

Where did that *come from?* Blythe wondered.

She got her answer as a pair of twins ran out from between the trees. It was Brittany and Whittany Biskit, better known as trouble times two!

"You and your stupid idea to go pumpkin picking, Brittany," Whittany grumbled. "Like, what's wrong with pumpkin in a can?"

Pumpkin picking? Blythe couldn't believe her ears. *The Biskits were doing something . . . fun?*

"Are you going to carve your pumpkin?" Blythe asked. "Or decorate it?"

"Does it look like we drink out of sippy cups?" Whittany snapped. "We were looking for the perfect pumpkin and we, like, found it."

"The Bag and Bean Café ran out of pumpkin lattes," Brittany explained. "Now they'll have no excuse!"

"I should have known." Blythe sighed.

The only idea of fun for the Biskits was making Littlest Pet Shop look bad. Their dad, Fisher Biskit, owned the competition, Largest Ever Pet Shop. The big box store had tons of space and merchandise but zero heart when it came to pets!

"We're going on a hayride," Blythe said. "Have you ever done that before?"

"And sit in straw with a stinky skunk and raccoon?" Whittany snorted at the wagon.

"Russell is a hedgehog,"

Blythe said.

"And I don't stink!" Pepper the skunk said for only Blythe to hear. "Well, most of the time."

The twins scowled at the pets chattering happily.

"Hayrides are for little kids," Whittany said. "We're super crazy close to being adults."

"Unlike you, baby Blythe," Brittany sniffed.

Blythe sighed and then said cheerily, "Enjoy your lattes."

Whittany and Brittany watched as the hayride continued up the path.

"Blythe and those creatures are having way too much fun," Whittany sneered. "But that is going to change."

"Like, how?" Brittany asked.

Whittany smiled slyly and said, "I think I know how to turn their hayride . . . into a STRAY ride!"

Chapter 2
Bad Sign

Blythe continued riding until she reached a sign showing where the trail was headed.

"That's weird," Blythe said. "The arrow is pointing into the wooded part of the park."

"Don't go in!" Sunil warned. "We could get poison ivy — or sprayed by a skunk!"

"You should be so lucky," Pepper snapped.

But the other pets were ready for adventure.

"The woods could inspire some beautiful songs!" Zoe said.

". . . Or just give us diseases," Sunil murmured.

Blythe smiled. "If the trail goes into the woods," she said, "so should we!"

The pets had no idea what to expect. They also had no idea they were being watched . . .

"Mission accomplished, Brittany," Whittany said as the twins popped up from behind the sign.

"Flipping that sign was, like, brilliant, Whittany. Blythe and those creatures will be lost and gone forever!"

"Speaking of gone," Brittany said, looking around. "Like . . . where's our perfect pumpkin?"

Meanwhile, Blythe pedaled the wagon deeper into the woods. She stopped when the path split in four directions.

"*Chillax*," Pepper declared. "I know a trusted scientific method of selecting the way to go."

Pepper pointed to each trail and said, "*Eenie, meenie, minie . . . mo!*"

"I'd go with *mo*," Vinnie told Blythe.

Blythe turned the wagon up the trail that Pepper picked. The forest grew thicker. The sky got darker.

When Blythe and the pets saw what was dangling from the trees, they gasped. There were spiderwebs!

Skeletons! And fluttery white ghosts!

"This isn't a hayride," Vinnie cried. "This is a hey-let's-get-out-of-here ride!"

Blythe looked around. "I would get us out of here if I could," she said slowly. "But I can't."

"Why not?" the pets asked together.

"Because," Blythe said, "I think we're lost!"

Chapter 3
Russell Says Relax!

"Lost?" Sunil cried.

"It's okay!" Blythe said. "I'll call for help on my phone."

But when Blythe grabbed her phone . . .

"That's weird," Blythe said, "the battery is drained, but I swear I charged it right before we left."

"I took some pictures with your phone, Blythe!" Minka said cheerily.

"Of the hayride."

"How many?" Blythe asked.

Minka began counting, "One . . . two . . . three . . . four hundred!"

"Four *hundred*?" Blythe cried.

"On to Plan B." Pepper sighed. "As in *bad news*!"

But Russell puffed out his chest and smiled.

"Maybe not!" Russell declared. "Lucky for you, you're riding with a former Wood Scout!"

"A *Wood* Scout?" Blythe asked.

"Wood Scouts learn how to survive in

the woods," Russell explained.

"Did you learn how to find your way *out*?" Zoe asked.

"I didn't earn my find-your-way-out-of-the-woods badge by roasting marshmallows!" Russell said.

"Super, Russell!" Blythe said with a smile. "What's the first thing we need to do?"

"The first thing we need to do is not panic," Russell said, "and stay relaxed."

"We can relax with some funny jokes!" Blythe suggested. "Pepper,

you're on!"

"I've got some jokes that go with the fall season," Pepper said. "Wait 'til you hear them!"

Blythe and the pets gathered around Pepper as she cracked her first joke:

"Where do monsters go when they're sick?" Pepper asked. "To a witch doctor!"

"Monsters? Witches?" Penny cried. "Where?"

"Why are vampires hard to get along with?" Pepper said. "Because they're pains in the neck!"

"Vampires?" Sunil cried. "Are they here, too?"

"What road is most haunted by ghosts?" Pepper joked. "A dead end!"

"Is that what we're lost on?" Zoe gasped.

Blythe frowned. Pepper's fall jokes were scary Halloween jokes and not good for keeping her and the pets relaxed.

"Any other suggestions, Russell?" Blythe sighed as she looked at the now-terrified pets.

Chapter 4
Masked Mystery

"Okay, everybody!" Russell said. "According to my Wood Scout training, we should use our five senses to navigate."

"Five senses," Blythe repeated. "Those are hearing, seeing, touching, tasting, and smelling."

"Being a dog, I have a great sense of smell!" Zoe said.

"Being a skunk, so do I," Pepper said. "Although, I don't want to brag."

"Zoe, you're up," Russell said. "Start sniffing for signs of something familiar."

"Gladly!" Zoe said. She pointed her nose in the air and sniffed. Her eyes lit up as she cried, "That's it!"

"Something that will get us out?" Blythe asked.

"No," Zoe said dreamily. "Something that will smell fabulous in my future signature perfume!"

Zoe sniffed the air again. "Is it honeysuckle? Jasmine? Help me out here, everyone."

"You were supposed to help *us*!" Pepper cried.

Blythe was about to calm everyone down when Penny shouted, "I smell popcorn!"

Blythe and the pets took a whiff. There was a faint smell of popcorn in the air!

"Maybe there's a movie theater nearby!" Blythe said hopefully. "Movie theaters are filled with people and are usually less spooky than this place!"

Blythe and the pets left the wagon to follow the scent. When they reached the end of the trail they didn't find a movie theater or people. They found a corn maze!

"There's the corn," Pepper said.

"Where's the *pop*?"

Blythe and the pets stared at rows and rows of straggly stalks. Standing among them was a scarecrow!

"Patched overalls . . . straw hands . . . tattered shirt," Sunil observed. "There's just one thing missing."

"What?" Penny asked.

"His head!" Sunil exclaimed.

A head suddenly rose above the scarecrow's shoulders. It had a floppy straw hat, a black mask over its eyes, and a grinning mouth that laughed, *"Mwa-ha-haaaaa!"*

"I think I smell trouble!" Zoe gulped. "That scarecrow is *alive*!"

Chapter 5
Follow the Leader

"Ahhhhhhhh!" Blythe and the pets screamed.

Terrified, they ran from the scarecrow but didn't get far. Soon they were lost inside the corn maze!

"What did they teach you in Wood Scouts about corn mazes, Russell?" Vinnie asked as they zigzagged around.

"To stay away from them!" Russell said.

After snaking through the maze, Blythe and the pets stumbled out, but they weren't out of the woods yet.

"That scarecrow is probably still around," Zoe said. "Let's get back to the wagon, Blythe."

"Good idea," Blythe said. "There's just one problem."

"What?" the pets asked.

"We lost our wagon!" Blythe sighed. "Let's just walk in a straight line!"

Russell suggested. "Sooner or later it will lead us out!"

"Yo!" Vinnie called out. "Who's up for Follow the Gecko?"

Blythe and the pets formed a line behind Vinnie. When they were in place, Vinnie led them in a neat straight line.

"This reminds me of something," Vinnie said.

"Something that will get us out of the woods?" Minka asked.

"Something that will make us DANCE!" Vinnie declared. "Everybody, CONGA!"

A conga beat filled the air as

Vinnie broke into fancy-footed dance steps. Soon the neat, straight line was squiggling in every direction!

"Vinnie, stop!" Blythe called.

But when Vinnie stopped, they were more lost than ever!

"I've seen straighter lines on coiled cobras!" Sunil complained.

Just then, Blythe spotted a field filled with round orange-colored objects.

"Vinnie did lead us somewhere," Blythe said. "To a pumpkin patch!"

Everyone inched closer to the pumpkins. Pumpkins stood in the middle of the patch piled on top of one another. The pumpkins had holes for arms and legs and the pumpkin on top was carved like a jack-o'-lantern. Atop the pumpkin pile sat a floppy straw hat and it looked a bit like —

"The spooky scarecrow!" Penny cried. "It's him!"

Chapter 6
Berry, Berry Scary

Blythe and the pets sprinted away from the pumpkin patch. They looked around and realized they were even more lost than before.

"I just had a terrible thought, as usual," Sunil cried. "What if we *never* find our way out?"

"Then someone will find *us*!" Russell said. "Wood Scouts learn how to leave signs that will catch the attention of rescuers."

"Like marking our turf?" Pepper asked, raising her tail. "Where do you want it?"

"The sign I mean is painting the word *HELP*!" Russell said.

"Minka is our artist!" Blythe said. She pointed to a boulder. "She can paint the sign on that big rock."

"I don't have paint!" Minka said.

"Use berries," Russell suggested. "Crushed berries make paint."

Quickly, Blythe and the pets went berry-picking in the shrubs nearby. They piled the berries next to Minka and stepped back.

"Ready, set, fling!" Russell shouted.

Minka flung the berries against the rock with a *SPLAT!* When she was done there were streaks, splotches, smudges, but no *HELP*.

"Why don't I write it?" Blythe suggested. Just then, something dropped from a tree.

"It's a spider," Russell said as they

gathered beneath the dangling bug.

"It might be a spider to you," Vinnie said. "But to me, it's dinner!"

Vinnie went to snatch the spider when *PLOP!* Something else dropped over Blythe and the pets. A web!

"Ahhhh!" Blythe and the pets screamed.

Now they were lost, and *trapped*!

Chapter 7
The Last Straw

Blythe and the pets pawed and clawed at the web, but they weren't quite strong enough to untangle themselves!

"Sorry, guys." Blythe sighed. "It was my dumb idea to take you on this hayride."

"It wasn't dumb, Blythe," Penny said. "You didn't know the hayride would turn into a scare-ride."

Suddenly, Blythe and the pets heard rustling leaves above them, and then a strange laugh.

They looked up. The masked scarecrow was sitting in the tree holding a rope attached to the web!

"Hey, you, stuffed shirt!" Pepper shouted bravely. "Get us out of here!"

"Okey dokey," the scarecrow said. He gave the rope a tug and the spiderweb flew up!

"We're free!" Minka cheered.

The scarecrow jumped down, grinned, and then was gone in the blink of an eye!

"No scary monster says *okey dokey*," Pepper said. "That guy is a fake!"

"Let's get him!" Vinnie shouted.

The chase was on!

"Why is he so short?" Zoe asked as they ran.

"Forget that," Vinnie said. "Why is he so *fast*?"

"I can fix that," Russell said. "Here's something else I learned."

Russell rolled himself into a tight ball and tumbled after the scarecrow.

"Go, Russell!" Blythe cheered.

Up ahead on the path, the scarecrow ran until he was halted by something blocking the way — the lost wagon!

The scarecrow backed up against the wagon as Russell rolled closer and closer. Until —

"Russ?" the scarecrow asked.

Russell popped out of his ball.

"Gus?"

"*Whaaat?* You two know each other?" Blythe cried, running to catch up.

Chapter 8
Fall for All!

Gus whipped off his mask and smiled. The scary scarecrow was a *raccoon*!

"That explains the mask," Pepper said. "Now explain how you know Russell."

"Russell and I were Wood Scouts together," Gus explained. "His nickname was Roly-Poly because of his awesome hedgehog roll. That's how I knew it was him."

"And your nickname is *Spooky*!" Blythe said angrily. "Why did you scare us?"

"Y-y-you talk to a-a-animals?" Gus screeched. *"Ahhhhhhhh!"*

"Get a grip, Gus!" Russell said, shaking his friend. "Blythe is cool!"

"She's right, too," Zoe said. "What were you thinking,

scaring us like that?"

"I built my spooky hayride trail years ago," Gus explained. "But no one was ever brave enough to ride into the wooded part of the park."

"You mean the park trail didn't even lead there?" Russell asked. "The sign pointed us in here."

Blythe narrowed her eyes as she remembered the Biskits. "Maybe someone turned the sign around," she said. "Some*one* . . . or *two*!"

The pets groaned.

"Maybe," Gus agreed. "But I'm glad you found my trail, even if it was spooky."

"Spooky? Ha!" Vinnie scoffed. "I come from hardy stock!"

"Chicken stock," Pepper muttered.

"You built the trail yourself, Gus?" Blythe asked. "The corn maze? The spiderweb? The glowing carved pumpkin?"

"I sure did," Gus confirmed.

Blythe smiled. Gus's ideas gave her one, too!

"Gus, how would you like to help us design a fall window display?" Blythe asked. "For the most fabulous pet shop in Downtown City?"

"That's Littlest Pet Shop!" Minka declared.

"Of course!" Gus exclaimed. "And I found the perfect pumpkin that would look great in your window! It came rolling in here a few hours ago."

"Cool!" Blythe said.

"This is all wonderful," Sunil said. "But perhaps Gus can do something else for us."

"What?" Gus asked.

"Get us out of these woods!" Sunil pleaded. "Pleeease!"

"Blythe, the Littlest Pet Shop fall window display is a hit!" Mrs.

Twombly declared a week later. "Who knew corn could be so stylish and —"

"A-maze-ing?" Blythe joked.

Mrs. Twombly hurried inside the store to help customers. Blythe and the pets heard a familiar, not-so-happy voice.

"What is the meaning of this, Blythe Baxter?"

Blythe cringed. Whittany and Brittany Biskit were glaring into the Littlest Pet Shop window!

"I spy with my little eye," Whittany sneered, "a perfect pumpkin!"

"Is that our perfect pumpkin-latte pumpkin?" Brittany demanded. "The one we, like, lost in the park? Wait, why aren't you lost in the park?"

Blythe smiled and said, "You'll have to ask our new window designer. His name is Gus."

Gus stepped out of the shop.

The twins gulped.

"Is Gus a . . . r-r-raccoon?" Whittany stammered.

"Raccoons have wicked sharp claws," Brittany said. "And wicked sharp —"

Gus flashed a grin.

"Teeth!!!" the twins screamed.

They kept screaming as they ran up the block and around a corner!

"We won't be seeing them for awhile,"

Blythe said. "And that's cool with me."

"Aren't you glad we went on that hayride through the park, Blythe?" Penny asked.

"Totally," Blythe said. "Not only did we find the most fabulous ideas for the Littlest Pet Shop fall window display . . ."

Blythe smiled at Gus and said, "We found the most fabulous new friend!"